J
SC

Sobol, Donald J.

Encyclopedia Brown
carries on

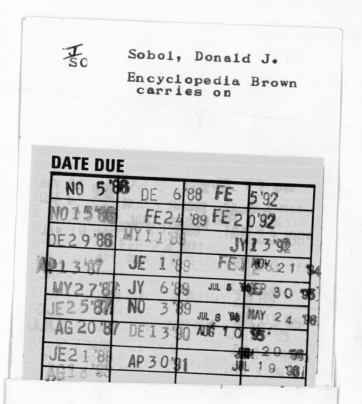

DATE DUE

NO 5'86	DE 6'88	FE 5'92
NO 15'86	FE 24 '89	FE 20'92
DE 29'86	MY 11'89	JY 13'92
AP 13'87	JE 1'89	FE 2 NOV 21 '94
MY 27'87	JY 6'89	JUL 5 '9 SEP 30 '95
JE 25'87	NO 3'89	JUL 8 '90 MAY 24 '96
AG 20'87	DE 13'90	AUG 1 0 '95
JE 21'88	AP 30'91	JUN 20 '96
AG 18'8		JUL 19 '96

© THE BAKER & TAYLOR CO

ENCYCLOPEDIA BROWN
CARRIES ON

ENCYCLOPEDIA BROWN CARRIES ON

by **DONALD J. SOBOL**

illustrations by IB OHLSSON

FOUR WINDS PRESS   **NEW YORK**

Library of Congress Cataloging in Publication Data

Sobol, Donald J
    Encyclopedia Brown carries on.

    Summary: Once again America's 10-year-old Sherlock Holmes in
sneakers is called upon to help his police-chief father and the neigh-
borhood children solve 10 mysteries.
    [1. Mystery and detective stories]   I. Ohlsson, Ib
II. Title.
PZ7.S68524Epa   [Fic]   79-6340
ISBN 0-590-07562-4

Published by Four Winds Press
A division of Scholastic Magazines, Inc., New York, N.Y.
Text copyright © 1980 by Donald J. Sobol
Illustrations copyright © 1980 by Scholastic Magazines, Inc.
Printed in the United States of America
Library of Congress Catalog Card Number: 79-6340
1 2 3 4 5 84 83 82 81 80

for Joan and Dick Dorff

Contents

The Case Of the Giant Mousetrap

Idaville!

Crooks turned pale at the mention of the town. They knew what to expect there — a fast trip to jail.

No one, grown-up or child, got away with breaking the law in Idaville.

Police across the nation wondered. How did Idaville do it? What was the secret behind its record of law and order?

Idaville looked like many other seaside towns. It had lovely beaches, three movie theaters, and four banks. It had churches, a synagogue, and two delicatessens.

And, of course, it had a police station. But that was not the real headquarters of the war on crime. A quiet red brick house on Rover Avenue was.

In the house lived Encyclopedia Brown, America's Sherlock Holmes in sneakers.

Mr. Brown, Encyclopedia's father, was chief of

1

police. He was brave and smart. But once in a while he came across a case that no one on the force could crack.

When that happened, Chief Brown knew what to do. He went home.

At the dinner table he told the facts to Encyclopedia. One telling was enough. Before the meal was over, Encyclopedia had solved the mystery for him.

Chief Brown was proud of his only child. He wanted it written in every school book: "The greatest detective in history wears sneakers to work."

But who would believe such a statement?

Who would believe that the brains behind Idaville's crime clean-up was ten years old? History wasn't ready for that.

So Chief Brown said nothing.

Encyclopedia never let slip a word about the help he gave his father. He didn't want to seem different from other fifth graders.

But there was nothing he could do about his nickname. He was stuck with it.

Only his parents and his teachers called him by his real name, Leroy. Everyone else called him Encyclopedia.

An encyclopedia is a book or set of books filled with all kinds of facts. Just like Encyclopedia's head.

Encyclopedia had read more books than anyone in Idaville, and he never forgot what he read. You might say he was the only library in America whose steps left footprints with a saw-toothed tread.

At the dinner table one Friday night, Chief Brown stirred his soup slowly. It was a sign that Encyclopedia and his mother knew well. A case was troubling him.

After a moment Chief Brown put down his spoon and said, "Salvatore Custer is at it again."

"Oh, no," groaned Encyclopedia.

Salvatore was an unemployed inventor and artist. He lived in Idaville six months of the year. The rest of the time he spent hanging his paintings in museums. Authorities removed them the instant they were discovered.

"Do you know the old saying, 'Build a better mousetrap and the world will beat a path to your door'?" asked Chief Brown. "Salvatore thought it said *bigger* mousetrap."

Chief Brown explained. Salvatore had built a mousetrap eight feet long, six feet wide, and five feet high. It had a motor and wheels, and it could go faster than a speeding mouse.

A museum of art in New York City had been interested for a while. But the museum had wounded Salvatore's pride. It had asked him to pay the shipping cost.

Next he had tried an exterminating company. He had thought the mousetrap would make good advertising. Turned down, he had parked his creation on the front lawn at City Hall.

"The problem," said Chief Brown, "is that no one

wants it there, and yet no one wants to move it. Salvatore won't drive it off—or rather, he's unable to. He hid the key and now he can't find it."

"How absolutely wild," said Mrs. Brown. "Why did he hide the key?"

"He was angry at the world for refusing his art," said Chief Brown, taking a notebook from his breast pocket. "Maybe you can help, Leroy. I wrote down everything Salvatore told me."

Using his notes, Chief Brown related what had happened.

About one o'clock that afternoon, Salvatore left the mousetrap in front of City Hall. "It's my gift to Idaville," he announced bitterly.

Just then a police car pulled up. Salvatore thought he was about to be arrested. Frightened, he fled into City Hall, hoping to escape through the rear exit.

In the lobby, he slipped on the marble floor. His head banged against a pillar. Dazed, he made his way unsteadily to the bank of elevators, which was nearer than the rear exit.

He remembered that in the subbasement there was a stairway that led up to Fourth Street at the side of the building. It seemed to him the best means of getting away.

As he rode dizzily down in the elevator, he grew angry. People had laughed enough at his art and inventions. He decided to strike back.

When he got off the elevator, he hid the ignition

key to the mousetrap. He put it in one of the trash boxes standing in a corner. If the police caught him, they would not find it.

The elevator car he had ridden was one of two that serviced the underground floor. He had just hidden the key when he saw the other elevator coming down. The police, he thought, were in full chase.

He was still dizzy, and he realized that he had no chance of outrunning his pursuers. So he decided not to use the stairs to Fourth Street.

He pressed the "up" button on the wall. The doors of his elevator opened, and he took it to the second floor. From there he hurried down the fire stairs to the ground floor and escaped out the rear exit.

Chief Brown closed his notebook. "That's about all of it," he said. "I found Salvatore at his sister's house. He was sorry about hiding the key, but it is too late."

"Why?" asked Mrs. Brown.

"The subbasement is the only floor that's cleaned out on Fridays. All the trash there—including the box with the key—was trucked to the dump and burned."

"Is the key really so important?" said Mrs. Brown. "Why can't the mousetrap be pushed off the lawn?"

Chief Brown chuckled. "When Salvatore hid the key, he may have been dizzy. But he was clearheaded about city government."

"I don't understand," said Mrs. Brown.

Chief Brown took a deep breath. "The police department won't touch the mousetrap. We claim it's the job of the department of parks. They say it's the job of the department of roads. It may be the job of the fire department or the dog pound. The mayor is looking up the law."

"Then the mousetrap will stay on the lawn for weeks," said Mrs. Brown.

Chief Brown nodded. "There the thing sits, right in the middle of town, waiting for a mouse the size of a dragon. It's Salvatore's revenge."

A long silence fell upon the room. Mrs. Brown glanced at Encyclopedia. He had not asked his one question. Usually he needed but one question to solve a case.

He had closed his eyes. He always closed his eyes when he did his heaviest thinking.

Suddenly his eyes opened. He asked his question.

"How many floors are there in City Hall, Dad?"

Chief Brown thought for a moment. "There's the subbasement at the bottom . . . and then the basement. Above ground are five floors."

"What does that have to do with the problem, Leroy?" asked Mrs. Brown. "The problem is to get the mousetrap moved."

"I just wanted to be certain there wasn't another floor below the subbasement," replied the boy detective.

His parents looked at him, puzzled.

"The key wasn't taken to the dump," said Encyclopedia. "It's still where Salvatore put it."

WHAT MADE ENCYCLOPEDIA SO SURE?

(Turn to page 61 for the solution to "The Case of the Giant Mousetrap.")

The Case of Bugs Meany,
Thinker

During the summer, Encyclopedia solved cases for the children of the neighborhood.

As soon as school let out, he set up a detective agency in the garage. Every morning he hung out his sign:

BROWN DETECTIVE AGENCY
13 Rover Avenue
Leroy Brown, President
No Case Too Small
25¢ Per Day
Plus Expenses

The first customer on Monday morning was Winslow Brant. Winslow was Idaville's master snooper. He snooped in trash piles all over town.

If he found something old and interesting, he fixed it up. Then he sold it at a flea market.

9

"I want to hire you," he said to Encyclopedia. "I think Bugs Meany smooth-talked me out of a cut-glass lamp."

Bugs Meany was the leader of a gang of tough older boys. They called themselves the Tigers. They should have called themselves the Elbow Bands. They were always up to something crooked.

"I found the lamp in Mrs. Bailey's trash last week," said Winslow. "It must be seventy-five years old and worth a lot to anyone who likes old lamps."

"Bugs stole it?" asked Encyclopedia.

"In a way," said Winslow. "I was taking it home when I met him. He told me he'd give me a Doctor of Philosophy diploma for it — if I was smart enough."

"Come again?" said Encyclopedia.

"Bugs tested my brains," Winslow went on. "He asked me: 'If Y equals Z times X, how long would it take a woodpecker to drill a hole through a kosher pickle?' I got the answer."

"You did?"

"I said the problem couldn't be solved without knowing the thickness of the pickle and the length of the woodpecker's beak. Bugs shook my hand. He said I could take his course in deep thinking."

Encyclopedia groaned. "On graduation, you'd get a Doctor of Philosophy diploma. And all Bugs wanted in return was the lamp."

"Right," said Winslow. "I thought of how proud my folks would be of their nine-year-old son the doctor. But I think Bugs put one over on me."

He laid twenty-five cents on the gas can beside Encyclopedia. "I want you to get back my lamp. Bugs said he'd return it if I wasn't completely satisfied with my progress."

"In that case, I'll see what I can do," replied Encyclopedia. He had handled Bugs and his Tigers in the past.

The Tigers' clubhouse was an unused toolshed behind Mr. Sweeney's Auto Body Shop. On the way there, Winslow explained about the deep-thinking course.

Bugs had told him to start slowly—say, one thought a day. After six weeks, a student should be having two-and-a-half thoughts a day. Even if they were always the same thoughts, they would be enough to earn a diploma as a Doctor of Philosophy.

When Encyclopedia and Winslow arrived at the Tigers' clubhouse, they found Bugs inside practicing his penmanship. He was learning to write excuse notes in his mother's handwriting.

"We came for Winslow's lamp," said Encyclopedia.

"Your thinking course is a big fat fake," added Winslow.

"What? What is this I hear?" gasped Bugs. "How is it possible? I myself got into deep thinking only three months ago. Already I am a new man."

"It hasn't done a thing for me," said Winslow.

"Perhaps you didn't heed my advice, dear lad," said Bugs, in a hurt voice. "If you put your mind to it, it will change your entire life and earn you a diploma."

"Just give me back my lamp," insisted Winslow.

Bugs lifted his gaze as though praying for patience.

"Did I try to sell you one of those new thinking caps, the ones with the orange and white racing stripes?" he asked. "No, no, no! All I asked was that you wear loose, comfortable clothes. And avoid tight shoes at all costs."

"You didn't have to sell me anything," said Winslow. "You took my lamp."

"Lamp?" exclaimed Bugs. "What lamp?"

"The cut-glass lamp I traded for your phoney course," said Winslow. "Maybe you forgot Mr. Stevens. He was cutting his grass when I handed the lamp to you. He saw us."

Bug's eyes squinted shut as though he'd been whacked on the nose.

"Don't faint on me," said Winslow.

"I was merely pausing in memory of all the sardines caught off the coast of Alaska," explained Bugs calmly.

"Huh?" muttered Winslow.

"Wait a second . . . . I seem to recall such a lamp," said Bugs. He breathed a sigh of regret. "Alas, it is no more."

"What happened to it?" demanded Encyclopedia.

"Sunday I was taking it to the flea market," said Bugs. "I was sitting with it in the cargo space of my uncle's truck. Suddenly the truck stopped for a traffic light—*screech!* The lamp flew back over the tailgate. It landed on the street—*smash!*

Bugs grinned at Encyclopedia, double-daring the boy detective to prove the story untrue.

Encyclopedia grinned back.

"Sorry, Bugs," he said. "You won't get me to fall for that one. Better take another course in deep thinking."

WHAT WAS BUGS'S MISTAKE?

(Turn to page 62 for the solution to "The Case of Bugs Meany, Thinker.")

The Case of the Grape Catcher

Bugs Meany thought a great deal about Encyclopedia's teeth.

The Tigers' leader longed to knock them so far that people a mile away would start dressing Christmas trees, thinking it was snowing.

Bugs hated being outsmarted time after time. He wanted to get even. But he didn't dare use muscle. Whenever he had that urge, he remembered Sally Kimball.

Sally was Encyclopedia's junior partner. She was also the prettiest girl in the fifth grade and the best athlete. More than once she had done the impossible. She had punched out Bugs Meany!

Because of Sally, Bugs never dared hit Encyclopedia. He never stopped planning his revenge, however.

"Bugs won't rest till he gets back at you, Encyclopedia," warned Sally.

"And at you," added Encyclopedia. "He tells everyone that he won't hit a girl. He says that he lets you win."

"Sour grapes," snorted Sally. "Speaking of grapes—my goodness!—I'm due at Edsel Wagonbottom's house right now. He wants me to pitch grapes to him."

Encyclopedia went with her. There was no way he would be left behind.

The Wagonbottoms owned a fruit company and lived in a large house on three acres. Edsel, a cocky fifth grader, met the detectives by the front steps. He held a bowl of grapes.

"I want to hire you for three or four hours," he said to Sally. "You have the best arm in school, and I use only the best."

He took the detectives around to the backyard. It was enclosed by thick hedges. In one corner stood a tennis court. Near the house was a swimming pool. Enough space was left over for a football field.

Edsel handed the bowl to Sally. "Throw me a grape," he said.

He jogged out twenty feet, hands at his sides, and turned. Sally forward-passed a green grape. Too low. Edsel lunged, missed.

"Don't throw on a straight line," he called impatiently. "Get more height."

Sally obeyed. After a few throws, she got the hang of it. Edsel caught every one in his mouth—glop, schlurp, swallow.

The day was very hot, and they took several

breaks. "I'd invite you to swim, but we just had the pool repaired," said Edsel. "It's still being filled."

Water was pouring from a pipe at one end of the pool and from a garden hose. The three children ran the cold water from the hose over their heads to cool off.

Then Sally resumed throwing. Edsel would race across the grass, turn, and wait for the throw, mouth open. He always made the play.

At the end of two hours, they stopped for lunch.

"The maid is off and my folks are away," said Edsel. "You'll have to eat frozen dinners."

While Sally and Encyclopedia fixed the meal, Edsel explained about his gifted mouth.

For two years he had performed at outings for the employees of his father's fruit company. But he had really come into his own earlier in the summer. The mayor had thrown out a grape to start the midget baseball league. It was a bad throw, but Edsel had caught it, no-handed.

"I'm ready to go nationwide," he boasted. "I'll be at the Fruit Growers meeting in Chicago next month. I figure to set an American record for boys—two hundred feet, hand to mouth."

After lunch, Edsel let Sally clean up the kitchen, and then they continued practicing. At two o'clock he brought out more grapes.

"Let's drill for quickness," he said. He turned off the garden hose and pulled the free end from the pool.

"Tie me up," he directed Encyclopedia. "I want to

practice catching without using my legs."

Encyclopedia tied Edsel with the hose. For a few minutes Sally threw from ten feet. Unable to move, Edsel missed frequently.

Suddenly Officer Carlson stepped into the backyard. Bugs Meany dashed out of the house.

"You see it, officer!" he screamed. "They're torturing this poor boy!"

The policeman looked uncertain.

"I came over to visit my pal, Edsel," Bugs went on. "What did I find? He was tied up like that. These two were hitting him with grapes and laughing. I had to call the police."

Officer Carlson untied Edsel. "Is this true?" he asked.

"It's true, I swear it!" gasped Edsel. He fell on the ground as if too weak to stand. "They tied me up and threw grapes at me for hours and hours."

"The inhuman fiends!" cried Bugs. "Torturing him in the hot, cruel sun! How he must have suffered!"

Edsel moaned. "They ganged up on me. Everyone knows what a dirty fighter the girl is. . . . Oooh. . . . Aaah."

"This is a frame-up!" Sally protested to Officer Carlson. "Bugs is trying to get us in trouble. He wants to get even. Edsel is helping him."

· "If he dies, I'll never forgive myself," blurted Bugs. "I shouldn't have waited for the police. I should have taken the law into my own hands."

"If you take anything, like one step closer, I'll knock you from under your dandruff," snapped Sally.

"You talk big," sneered Bugs. "But you're not fooling anyone. The heat is finally on *you.*"

"Wrong, Bugs," said Encyclopedia. "I can prove the heat isn't where it should be."

WHAT DID ENCYCLOPEDIA MEAN?

(Turn to page 63 for the solution to "The Case of the Grape Catcher.")

The Case of the Left-Handers Club

Daisy Pender walked into the Brown Detective Agency. Across her T-shirt was printed "Left is Right."

"I'm on my way to the meeting of the Idaville Left-Handers Club," she said. "We're going to name our Left-Hander of the Year and draw up our Bill of Rights . . . er, Lefts."

"I heard you had trouble at the last meeting," said Encyclopedia.

"And how," replied Daisy. "Somebody slipped castor oil into the fruit punch. That's why I'm here. I'm worried."

She pitched a quarter onto the gas can beside Encyclopedia.

"Today's meeting is at the high school cafeteria in half an hour," she said. "I want to hire you to watch things. I'll help, of course. I'm practicing to be a detective myself."

She pointed to Encyclopedia's feet.

"You've been on a murder case," she declared. "Your sneakers are covered with blood stains."

The "blood stains" were ketchup drops.

"You're some detective, Daisy," said Encyclopedia with a straight face.

Out by the bikes, Sally whispered, "If she opens her own detective agency, I have the perfect name — Daisy's Disaster."

"She means well," whispered back Encyclopedia.

On the ride to the meeting, Daisy told the detectives about the Left-Handers Club. It had been founded by a group of concerned young men and women.

Members fought for equal opportunity in jobs and in dealing with a right-handed world of pencil sharpeners, auto gear shifts, TV controls, and telephone booths.

"One out of every ten Americans is left-handed," said Daisy. "We won't be left out, left behind, or left over."

"Sounds reasonable," admitted Encyclopedia.

"But someone is trying to break up the club," said Daisy. "I guess we made a lot of enemies because we want to be allowed to shake with our left hands."

Encyclopedia was still thinking that one over when they reached the high school. About sixty men and women were in the cafeteria.

The boy detective posted Sally and Daisy by the side doors.

"What am I looking for?" asked Daisy.

"Anything suspicious," answered Encyclopedia. It was the best he could do on an empty stomach.

Happily, the meeting was called to order. Encyclopedia took up a position by the main entrance.

The club members talked over their Bill of Lefts. During the discussion, three young men departed from the room. They went separately, using Daisy's door, and returned separately. None was gone more than a few minutes.

Suddenly Encyclopedia heard police sirens. Officer Feldman entered the cafeteria. He carried a rifle.

"Remain where you are, everyone," he said calmly but firmly. "We got a telephone call that a lion has escaped from the zoo. The caller said he saw the animal enter this building."

Several girls screamed. Encyclopedia hoped the screams would drown out his knees, which were beating out "Jingle Bells."

Officer Feldman said, "The caller wouldn't give his name. So this whole thing might be a false alarm. We're checking the zoo. In the meantime, please stay here and keep cool."

"A lion on the loose, my foot!" said Daisy. "It's just a trick to break up the meeting!"

"Whoever called had to be here in the school," said Sally. "His timing was too perfect. He waited until the meeting started."

"You might be right," said Encyclopedia. "Three

men were out of the room at one time or another. What are their names, Daisy?"

"Joe Evans, who left first. Then Mike Dent, and then Bill Stevens," replied Daisy.

Encyclopedia said, "The door they used leads to the hall with the washrooms—"

"And the public telephone!" exclaimed Sally.

"Each of the three men was alone long enough to make the call," said Encyclopedia.

"Joe Evans is the one," said Daisy. "He's strange. One of his hands is lighter in color than the other."

"Joe plays golf with my father," said Sally. "He wears a glove on his right hand. That's why it's lighter. It's not as sunburned as his left hand."

"Then the one who called must be Mike Dent," said Daisy. "He's real strange, too. One of his ears is lower than the other."

"What?" muttered Sally. She walked past Mike, studying his ears out of the corner of her eye.

"It isn't his ears," she reported. "It's the hair growing down his temples—his sideburns. They're uneven. The left sideburn is longer than the right."

Daisy wasn't discouraged. "Then the caller must be Bill Stevens," she insisted. "He was the last to leave the room. And talk about *strange!* His legs are too long."

Sally circled Bill Stevens, who was talking to Officer Feldman. She returned and said, "His legs aren't too long. His pants are too short. You're some help, Daisy!"

Daisy stiffened. "If that's the way you feel, you can solve this case by yourselves. I quit!"

"Phew," said Sally, as Daisy marched off. "Now we can get to work. Only I don't know where to begin."

"Begin with the best suspect," suggested Encyclopedia.

"But which one?" asked Sally. "Do you know?"

"I think so," replied the boy detective.

WHOM DID ENCYCLOPEDIA SUSPECT?

(Turn to page 65 for the solution to "The Case of the Left-Handers Club.")

The Case of the Diving Partner

Otis Dibbs biked up to the Brown Detective Agency. He wore sneakers and a bathing suit, and he was dry all over.

Otis was usually soaking wet. During the summer he dived for golf balls that had been hit into the water hazards on Idaville's two golf courses. He sold the balls to golfers who liked to use old balls near the water.

The work had its dangers. Golfers sometimes mistook him for an alligator. They waited to bop him on the head with a club when he came up for air.

"Golly, Otis," said Encyclopedia. "What are you doing here? You're way off course."

"I want to hire you," said Otis. He placed twenty-five cents on the gasoline can beside the boy detective. "Helga the Horrible—I mean, Helga Smith—is taking over my business."

26

"That lazy windbag?" exclaimed Sally. "Every night she must dream she found a job. She looks tired even in the morning."

"The only time Helga lifts a finger is when Miss Casey tells her to," said Encyclopedia.

Miss Casey was the manicurist at the Ace Beauty Parlor. She did Helga's nails every week.

"Helga muscled in on my business," said Otis. "I do all the work, but she takes half the money."

"We'll look into it," said Sally. "Where is she?"

"I left her at the sixth hole of the country club half an hour ago," said Otis.

The three children got their bikes. Otis talked about the case as they pedaled to the country club.

Diving for golf balls was hard work, but worth the effort. Golfers always needed cheap balls to use on water holes.

Also, Otis found a lot of clubs, which angry golfers threw into the water. Putters were the most common. But once in a while he found a complete, matched set.

The business of selling the old balls and clubs had been good until last week. Then Helga came by and gave him some advice.

"She slapped me on the back and told me how much better I'd do with her as a partner."

"The slap on the back was to help you swallow what she said," grumbled Sally.

"You know it," agreed Otis. "You've got to get rid of that big do-nothing."

"We'll find a way," promised Encyclopedia. "Don't worry."

But Encyclopedia worried. Helga was seventeen and could have gone to a reform school on a scholarship. She had a grin like a saber-toothed tiger.

At the country club, Otis showed them where to park their bikes. Then they walked quickly to the sixth hole.

Helga was just climbing out of the pond to the right of the fairway. She wore an orange bathing suit and goggles. She waved to Otis and pointed to a sign near the water.

CAUTION: DIVERS AT WORK

"How do you like it?" she called. "It was delivered a few minutes ago. What a work of art! Cost us only twenty dollars, little partner."

Otis gagged. "T-twenty d-dollars?"

Encyclopedia stared at the sign. It looked as if it had been painted on the back of a motorcycle.

"Otis doesn't need a sign," snapped Sally. "And he doesn't need a partner."

"Wrong, my dear," replied Helga. "With both of us diving, we can double our business."

"You haven't dived *once!*" protested Otis. "All you do is lie in the shade and count the balls I bring up. But when I sell them, you grab half the money."

"Temper, temper," Helga warned. She tapped the

thick, smooth tips of her fingers together. Then she made a show of examining her manicured nails.

Encyclopedia looked from Helga to the only shaded place near the pond — a clump of six oak trees.

"Helga could have been resting there, waiting for Otis to return," thought the boy detective. "She could have seen us before we saw her. All she would have had to do was slip into the water and pretend she'd been busy diving."

"A business," Helga said, "has to be run with brains. Now, take the sign. Golfers won't mistake us for alligators anymore. That's thinking the Helga Smith way."

"Fore!" a man shouted from the fifth tee. "Fore!"

"Duck!" cried Otis. A ball whizzed past Encyclopedia and splashed into the pond.

"Go get it, partner," commanded Helga.

"Why don't you?" said Sally.

"I'm tired out," Helga answered. "I've been diving for a solid hour." She nodded at a green pail beside Otis's clothes. "Found nine balls and a putter while you were gone."

"I found the putter and those balls this morning!" screamed Otis.

"Are you calling me a liar?" Helga rose slowly to her feet, breathing heavily on her right fist.

Otis retreated five steps, just breathing heavily.

"Nobody calls me a liar," said Helga. "You prove I didn't find those balls, and I'll bow out. You can have the business all to yourself."

"And if he can't prove you lied?" demanded Sally.

Encyclopedia wished Sally hadn't asked the question.

"If he can't," repeated Helga, grinning her saber-toothed-tiger grin. "If he can't, I'll find myself another partner. And I'll flatten this one's nose till it looks like an all-day pizza."

Otis uttered a low moan.

"Encyclopedia," said Sally, "help Otis!"

"You mean prove that Helga didn't dive for those balls?" inquired the boy detective. "That's easy."

WHAT WAS THE PROOF?

(Turn to page 66 for the solution to "The Case of the Diving Partner.")

The Case of the Upside-Down Witness

Elton Fisk hurried into the Brown Detective Agency. He had his feet on the ground.

About this time every summer, Elton usually had his feet stuck in the air. He raised money for the General Hospital by standing on his head all over town. People tossed coins into his cap.

"You know the three men who held up the bank yesterday?" he said. "I saw them. But I forget where."

"You *forget?*" cried Sally. "Elton, you've spent too much time standing on your brains."

"My brains are fine," insisted Elton. "It's just that I didn't know about the holdup until I read the newspaper this morning. What I saw yesterday didn't seem important at the time."

"What *did* you see?" asked Encyclopedia.

"Three men in yellow coveralls ran into a store,"

said Elton. "They didn't have masks. But they were carrying paper bags."

Encyclopedia jumped to his feet. "Three men in masks and yellow coveralls held up the First National Bank yesterday afternoon," he said. "They stuffed the money into paper bags."

"They probably hid the masks as soon as they were away from the bank," said Sally.

"Don't you remember anything about the store they went into?" asked Encyclopedia.

"It was downtown," replied Elton. "And it had a big sign in the window—a white sign with black letters."

"What was written on the sign?" asked Sally.

"A lot of words. But I could read two of them," Elton said proudly.

"What's so great about reading two words?" demanded Sally.

"Look," said Elton, "I was standing on my head. I had to read the sign upside down. And come to think of it, *backward,* too!"

He explained. He had been looking into a large mirror when he saw the robbers enter a store across the street.

"Last week Bugs Meany and his Tigers gave me a hotfoot while I was doing a headstand," he said. "So I set up a large mirror to keep them from sneaking up behind me."

"The store with the sign must be a hideout," put in Encyclopedia thoughtfully.

"Finding the store should be a cinch," said Sally. "All we have to do is spot a sign with the two words Elton read."

"I forget what they are," Elton said lamely.

Gloom fell upon the Brown Detective Agency.

Finally Sally said, "Never mind. Some store window has a sign that's wrong. Two words are written upside down and backward."

"That's the answer!" whooped Elton. "Words appearing upside down and backward to someone walking past would look just right if you stood on your head and read them in a mirror."

"The two words were probably stuck in as a stunt to catch the eye," said Sally.

"We're wasting breath talking," said Elton. "We should be looking."

Since Elton could not remember all the streets he'd been on, Encyclopedia decided to comb every one in the downtown area.

The first black-and-white sign they came to was in the window of Slattery's Fish Market on Monroe Street.

CHOICE	COD
	BLUE
Of Any 3 Fish	KING
	DOLPHIN
For the Price of 2	FLOUNDER

"Every word is plain as day," said Sally.

They moved on, looking for a sign with two words upside down and backward. They reached Dwight's Men's Store. A black-and-white sign in the window read:

BARGAINS! BARGAINS!
Everything Must Go
Shirts, Slacks, Suits
Our Loss Is Your Gain

"No luck," said Elton. "I wish I hadn't moved around so much yesterday. I did handstands in dozens of places."

"Don't be discouraged," said Sally cheerfully. "We've lots of streets to check."

For the next two hours they peered at shop windows. First they walked the east-west streets. Then they walked the north-south streets.

They saw no other black-and-white window signs until they arrived at Highland Avenue, the last street.

In the window of Meleger's Furniture Store was the sign:

SUMMER SALE!
Three-Piece Bedroom Set
Only $399

Four doors away, the window of McDuffy's Shoe

Store bore the sign:

PRICES SLASHED!
Up to 50% Off
SAVE SAVE SAVE

"We're out of store windows," said Elton glumly. "We'll never find the store the robbers entered."

"They might have taken the sign down," said Sally. "Encyclopedia, can't you think of something?"

"I've already thought of something," replied the boy detective. "We've been looking at this case in the wrong way. The robbers went into—"

WHICH STORE?

(Turn to page 67 for the solution to "The Case of the Upside-Down Witness.")

The Case of the Marvelous Egg

Chester Jenkins swept past the Brown Detective Agency. He was carrying an egg.

Encyclopedia and Sally glanced questioningly at each other. Chester hurried nowhere except to the refrigerator.

Furthermore, Chester carried food to one place only—his mouth. He was well known as a fork on foot.

"Hey, Chester," Encyclopedia called. "What's the big hurry?"

Chester stopped. "Egg power," he said. "Egg power is going to make us kids independently wealthy. Wilford Wiggins says so."

Wilford Wiggins was a high school dropout and too lazy to scratch. His only exercise was watching monster movies on television and letting his flesh crawl.

He spent most of his waking hours dreaming up

get-rich-quick schemes. Encyclopedia had stopped him many times from cheating the children of the neighborhood.

"Wilford has called a secret meeting at the city dump for two o'clock today," said Chester. "He told us kids to bring an egg and all our money. He promised to explain everything."

"Wilford didn't tell me about the secret meeting," said Encyclopedia.

"He must be afraid you'll shoot him down again," said Chester. Suddenly his face clouded. "Say, maybe I'd better hire you to come along—just in case."

"It's nearly two o'clock now," said Sally. "Let's go."

They arrived at the dump as the meeting was starting. Wilford stood on a burnt table. Beside him was a tall boy dressed in a crash helmet, goggles, and a jumpsuit. Strapped to his back was a parachute.

The detectives and Chester moved in quietly. They found places at the rear of the crowd of eager children.

"It's terrible," whispered Chester. "Everyone is money mad—including me."

Wilford raised his hands for quiet.

"I see you've all brought an egg," he said. "Good. Now take a look at your egg. What do you see?"

He let the children stare at their eggs for a moment. Then he said, "Every egg has the same shape—round!"

"You got us out here to say *that?*" shouted Bugs Meany. "If you went completely out of your mind, no one would know the difference."

"Calm down, kiddo," growled Wilford. "I ought to get angry and not allow you in on the big money-making deal I have for all the faithful."

"Well, what egg isn't round?" snarled Bugs.

Wilford chuckled mysteriously. He reached into his pocket and brought out a small box.

"The egg inside this box isn't round," he announced. "It's *square!*"

Gasps rose from the crowd, plus one shout of disbelief. It was Bugs again.

"Man, oh, man!" cried the Tigers' leader. "When you go to the zoo, you must buy two tickets—one to get in and one to get out!"

Wilford ignored the wisecrack. "Think of what eggs shaped like square blocks will mean to America—to the world!" he said.

The children considered the possibilities. Their doubts gradually turned to wonder as they thought about it. What a gift to mankind!

"Square eggs won't roll off the table," offered Charlie Stewart.

"You can slice them and use them on sandwiches and not waste the bread corners," sang Otto Beck.

The children chattered about the possibilities. They saw a fortune at their fingertips.

"Others have made square eggs," admitted Wilford. "But they had to boil the egg, remove the shell, and then squeeze the egg into a square block. That's not what will make us millions. No, siree!"

Wilford threw back his head triumphantly. "I've done it! Me, Wilford Wiggins! I've bred chickens that lay square eggs!"

The youth with the parachute spoke. "You're asking yourselves if a square egg will break too easily. And you want to know why Wilford doesn't show you the egg inside the small box."

"I'll tell you," said Wilford. "I'm a man of my word. I promised the newspaper and television people not to show anyone the world's first square egg before they see it.

"A lot of bigshots are waiting at the airport right now," he went on. "This young man beside me is Buddy Stilwell, a skydiver. He hopes to take off in half an hour. You can see that he's dressed and ready to jump."

Buddy Stilwell said, "I'll drop from twenty thousand feet holding the square egg in my hand. When I parachute to a landing, I'll show the reporters and the cameras the egg—unbroken! The news will flash around the earth. People everywhere will demand strong, square eggs."

"I'm asking you to trust me," said Wilford. "But I can't lie. I spent all my money developing my sensational chickens. I need your dollars to rent the airplane."

"The minute we rent it," said Buddy Stilwell, "that's the minute the egg and I soar into the sky."

"Right," said Wilford. "So I'm offering all my young friends a chance to strike it rich. For five dollars, each of you can buy a share of the biggest opportunity in history."

The children took out their money. They lined up excitedly to buy shares.

"Encyclopedia," said Sally. "You can't let all these kids fall for Wilford's fast talk."

"Fall is the right word," said Encyclopedia.

WHAT WAS WILFORD'S MISTAKE?

(Turn to page 68 for the solution to "The Case of the Marvelous Egg.")

The Case of the Overfed Pigs

Although Lucy Fibbs was only nine, she was already a swimming teacher. She didn't teach children. She taught pigs.

The job was not all glory. Wednesday morning Lucy telephoned Encyclopedia with a weighty problem.

"Someone is secretly fattening my pigs so they'll sink instead of swim," she said.

"Oh, my achin' bacon," thought Encyclopedia. "What next?"

"You've got to find out who is doing it!" exclaimed Lucy.

"I'll be right over," promised Encyclopedia.

He and Sally caught the number 9 bus. They rode to the farming country north of town. Lucy met them at the stop near her house.

"I'll show you around first," she said. "We can start in the pig barn."

Over the barn door was written: "Through These

44

Doors Pass the Fastest Racing Pigs in the World."

"Pigs are smart," said Lucy, herding four young ones into a chute. "Watch."

She yanked open the starting gate. The four pigs dashed on a four-second sprint to a feed bowl fifty feet away.

"A man in Iowa is planning to hold the first All-Pig Olympics next summer," said Lucy. "I'm going to enter a team."

"Won't these pigs be too big and slow by next summer?" inquired Sally.

"Sure they will," replied Lucy. "I'm just practicing on them—learning how to train for speed. Maybe I'll cut the workouts down to two a day."

"You don't want them to keel over from teaching you," agreed Encyclopedia.

"By next summer, I should have a few sprinters that can go fifty feet in three seconds flat," said Lucy. "That's about equal to a five-minute mile, you know."

"Do you train them to swim at the same time?" asked Sally.

"Golly, no," said Lucy. "The runners are Hampshires. The swimmers are Yorkshire Whites. Come along and you'll see."

She led the detectives to a small swimming pool surrounded by a wire fence. Near the pool several whitish pigs snoozed in the sun.

"You have to start the swimmers when they're two or three days old," she said. "First you teach them to drink milk from a baby bottle. Then you lead them to the water. Soon they dive to get the bottle. In six weeks, splasho! They're swimming."

"Breaststroke or crawl?" asked Encyclopedia.

"Piggypaddle," answered Lucy.

The pigs, the detectives learned, performed four shows daily at Submarine World in nearby Dade Springs. They had a ten-minute act that included perfect "swine" dives.

"My sister Carol dreamed up the act four years ago," said Lucy. "She works with the pigs at the show. I stay here and look after training. I have to have understudies ready to replace overweight swimmers."

"And someone is helping them to gain weight?" said Sally.

"I'm sure of it," said Lucy. "Usually, pigs can perform until they are two years old. At that age, they weigh about a hundred pounds. If they are heavier, they tire in the water. They sink and can drown."

Lucy told the detectives that last month several pigs were found swimming too low in the water. Her sister Carol put them on the scale. They were twenty to thirty pounds overweight!

"They must have been fed on the sly for weeks," said Lucy. "Somebody is trying to put us out of business."

"Why should anyone do that?" asked Sally.

"Jealousy, I guess," said Lucy. "Lots of farmers

would like their pigs to be swimming stars."

"They must hog the show at Submarine World," said Sally.

Encyclopedia winced. Then he said, businesslike, "Where do your swimmers sleep at night?"

"In the rear of the pig barn," answered Lucy. "My sister trucks them back and forth to the show each day."

"The barn isn't very safe," said Sally. "Anyone could sneak in."

"I think someone did last night," replied Lucy.

She explained. Her family had returned from the movies late at night. As they drove up, they spied the kitchen lights on. Then they saw a teen-ager run out the back door.

"We didn't get a good look at him," said Lucy. "He moved too fast."

There was more. Lucy's father later questioned the neighbors. One of them, Mr. Brandt, had seen two cars, one towing the other, not far from Lucy's house.

"That was about half an hour after we returned from the movies," said Lucy. "It was too dark for Mr. Brandt to see the cars clearly."

Lucy had a second clue.

"Dad found a slip of paper on the kitchen floor," she said. "He gave it to the police. It had two words typed on it: *pig iron.*"

"*Pig . . . iron . . .*" Encyclopedia repeated to himself.

To Lucy, he said, "Where are the telephones in your house?"

"There is only one," replied Lucy. "It's in the kitchen."

"Good. It all fits," said Encyclopedia.

"You mean you know who has been fattening Lucy's swimmers?" gasped Sally.

"Not yet," said Encyclopedia. "But the police shouldn't have much difficulty finding out who he is."

WHY WAS ENCYCLOPEDIA SO SURE?

(Turn to page 69 for the solution to "The Case of the Overfed Pigs.")

The Case of the Ball of String

Encyclopedia and Sally visited the Children's Hobby Show at the junior high school two hours before it opened. Cosimo Bender had asked them to hurry over.

Cosimo was waiting by the flagpole. "The show is being set up in the west wing," he told the detectives. "I've entered a ball of string."

"Say that again, please?" requested Sally.

"String," said Cosimo, squaring his shoulders. "My ball is nearly two-and-a-half feet across. It has a good chance of winning the Collecting for Fun prize."

Cosimo explained. The Collecting for Fun category was a new one at the hobby show.

"Nothing entered in Collecting for Fun can be worth trading or selling," he said. "It has to be — well, junk."

"Is Ralph Stockton showing his broken golf tees?" asked Sally.

"In sixty-six different colors," said Cosimo. "Bubba Ludwig entered his corks. Jim Sunshine brought his blown light bulbs, no two alike. There are four other great collections, but my ball of string is the favorite."

The children walked into the west wing of the school. In classrooms on both sides of the hall, boys and girls were busy setting up their exhibits.

"I want to hire you," said Cosimo. "I'm worried."

"What about?" asked Encyclopedia.

"Someone is trying to stop me from winning," answered Cosimo. "A rumor is floating around that my string is a fake—that it has a basketball in the center."

"How rotten!" exclaimed Sally.

"My ball is true string, through and through," insisted Cosimo. "Oh, it has a little bit of wrapper twine and some binder twine. And maybe a few acorns, but—"

"Acorns?" repeated Sally.

"I keep the ball in the backyard where I can look at it whenever I want to," said Cosimo. "Squirrels like to sit on it. They can't sit on a two-and-a-half-foot ball of string just anywhere."

The children had come to a large door at the end of the hall. Above the door was a sign: "Room 9— COLLECTING FOR FUN."

The room was small, and crowded with eight tables. Collections of useless objects were spread lovingly upon seven of the tables. The eighth table was bare.

"My ball of string!" wailed Cosimo. "It's been stolen!"

A narrow door stood in the back wall of the room. It led, Encyclopedia discovered, to the grounds behind the school.

The boy detective's brain raced. Whoever stole the ball of string probably took it out the back door. The thief wouldn't have dared to use the large door to the hall. Too many children would have seen him.

Cosimo was in shock. So Encyclopedia sent Sally to search the grounds. Then he examined the room carefully.

The table from which the string had been stolen drew his attention. The top of the table was marked with scratches about half an inch long. He found similar scratches on the floor of the back doorway.

Encyclopedia borrowed a ruler from the office and measured both sets of scratches.

The table had six scratches in a line. The first five were almost exactly $6 \frac{1}{8}$ inches apart. The sixth was $4 \frac{1}{2}$ inches from the scratch before it.

The scratches in the doorway were the same. Only the last scratch, instead of being $4 \frac{1}{2}$ inches from the one before it, was $5 \frac{1}{2}$ inches away.

"So that's it!" murmured the boy detective.

He read the name cards beside each collection. Four of the boys were his friends. The other three— Tom Gelb, John Morgan, and Charles Frost, he had never met.

By now Cosimo had recovered himself. He was

able to tell Encyclopedia a little about each of the three boys. All of them had a hobby beside the one displayed in the Collecting for Fun room.

Tom Gelb was ten. He built model ships. His model of the *Queen Mary* was on exhibit in room 5. He was a good math student.

John Morgan was eleven. He had the best collection of rare money—bills and coins—of any boy in Idaville. He knew everything there was to know about money minted after 1900.

Charles Frost was twelve but looked fourteen. His collection of baseball cards was in room 6. He was not a good student, but he shone at sports and art.

"Do you know who the thief is?" asked Cosimo.

"I have a pretty good idea," said Encyclopedia. "But I must be sure. Here's what I want you to do."

He instructed Cosimo to gather all the boys in the Collecting for Fun group. After asking their help in solving the theft, Cosimo was to mention the lone clue: the scratches spaced 6 $\frac{1}{8}$ inches apart.

Within half an hour, Cosimo had the boys assembled in room 9. He closed the door.

As Encyclopedia waited in the hall, Sally returned.

"I looked all over the grounds," she said glumly. "I didn't find the ball of string."

A few minutes later Cosimo came out.

"Your plan fell on its face," he said to Encyclopedia. "I spoke about the scratches and pointed out that most of them were 6 $\frac{1}{8}$ inches apart. But no one had any idea what that meant."

"Perfect," said Encyclopedia. "The thief has to be—"

WHO IS THE THIEF?

(Turn to page 71 for the solution to "The Case of the Ball of String.")

The Case of the Thermos Bottle

On Saturday, Encyclopedia and Sally biked to the elementary school.

The Parent-Teacher Association was holding its summer carnival. Money from the ticket sale would help buy a new air-conditioner for the cafeteria.

The detectives each bought a dozen tickets. They had started down a row of booths when they heard Benny Breslin calling to them.

They turned toward the athletic field. A large crowd had gathered to watch the chicken-flying contest. Benny had emerged from the crowd and was fast approaching them. He had a hen under one arm.

"What happened to the worm race?" Sally asked him.

"It's been dropped," said Benny. "Too many kids stepped on opponents' worms last year."

Encyclopedia remembered. Bugs Meany alone

had stepped on five worms. Bugs had been boiling mad. He had painted a caterpillar to look like a worm. But the day of the race, it turned into a butterfly. His worm, Fast Ernie, finished next to last.

"How are you doing, Benny?" inquired Sally.

"Queen Cluck here is leading," answered Benny, patting his hen. "If she holds form in the finals, I'll win. First prize is two tickets to the Crest Theater."

"Has Bugs entered a hen?" asked Encyclopedia.

"If he has, it's probably a baby eagle with its claws trimmed," said Sally.

As she spoke, Bugs and several of his Tigers came out of the school. Bugs was carrying a large green thermos bottle, the kind Encyclopedia's mother filled with a hot or cold drink and took on picnics.

"I smell a rat," said Sally.

"Uh-uh," said Benny. "Bugs is trying to make up for being such a poor sport last year. He got Adler's Sporting Goods Store to donate a baseball glove. He's holding a drawing for it at noon."

"I don't trust him," insisted Sally. "Bugs stands for everything he thinks you'll fall for."

"He can't pull any tricks today," said Benny. "Too many parents are here."

A whistle blew. Mr. Pardee, a fifth-grade teacher, called for the finalists in the chicken-flying contest.

"Boys and girls," he shouted. "Prepare to start your chickens!"

The detectives wished Benny happy landing. They should have spoken to the hen. Queen Cluck refused to come out of the starting pad, a mailbox.

Benny pleaded. Benny coaxed. Benny poked her gently with a toilet plunger.

After two minutes, Queen Cluck came out— backward. A hen named Juliet won with a flight of 137 feet, 9 inches.

"Maybe I'll win the baseball glove," said Benny glumly.

The detectives followed him to a table near the library door, where Bugs Meany and his Tigers were selling chances. The baseball glove rested on the table beside a can of root beer.

Benny gave Bugs two tickets and received a slip of paper with a number on it. Bugs wrote the same number on a Ping-Pong ball. He dropped the ball into a box made of clear plastic.

Something bothered Encyclopedia. The green thermos bottle stood under Bugs's chair—yet Bugs sipped from the can of root beer.

"I just made it," said Benny to Encyclopedia. He clutched his slip of paper with the number 114 on it. "I bought the last chance."

It was noon and time for the drawing.

Bugs strutted in front of the plastic box. "I've asked Miss Spottswood to blindfold my buddy, Duke Kelly," he announced.

Miss Spottswood, the school nurse, and Duke Kelly made their way through the crowd. Miss Spottswood wrapped a strip of heavy white cloth around Duke's eyes.

"Watch closely, everybody," sang Bugs. "Are you ready, Duke?"

"Ready," replied the blindfolded Duke. He raised both hands to show they were empty.

Bugs was quick to call attention to Duke's short sleeves. "Nothing is up them," he sang. "Duke Kelly is one boy you can trust!"

"Horsefeathers," snorted Sally. "Duke is so crooked he has to screw on his hat."

Miss Spottswood guided Duke's right hand to the box of Ping-Pong balls. He felt around for a full minute.

"Duke is stirring up the balls," Bugs explained to the crowd. "We don't want you to think the winning ball is stuck on top."

Duke suddenly pulled out a ball. Ripping off his blindfold, he held up the ball so everyone could read the number — 81.

"Do you all see it?" screamed Bugs. "Eighty-one! Who's won himself this beautiful major-league baseball glove?"

"Me!" shouted Rick Larsen. He rushed up to Miss Spottswood and showed her his slip with "81" on it. She gave him the baseball glove and shook his hand.

"It's a gyp," exclaimed Sally. "Rick Larsen is Bugs's pal."

Encyclopedia didn't answer. He was staring thoughtfully at the large green thermos bottle under Bugs's chair.

Sally stamped the ground. "Encyclopedia! If you

can't prove the drawing was fixed, Bugs will end up with the baseball glove himself!"

"No, he won't," said Encyclopedia. "He should never have sipped from the can of root beer. He forgot the thermos bottle was in plain view."

WHAT DID ENCYCLOPEDIA MEAN?

(Turn to page 72 for the solution to "The Case of the Thermos Bottle.")

Solution to "The Case of the Giant Mousetrap"

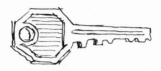

Salvatore was still dizzy when he got into the elevator to go from the lobby to the subbasement. He pushed the wrong button—and got off at the wrong floor.

After hiding the key, he opened the elevator doors again by pushing the "up" button on the wall.

That was Encyclopedia's clue.

The subbasement was the bottom floor, and bottom floors do not have "up" and "down" buttons by the elevators. They have one button only.

Encyclopedia realized that the key was still where Salvatore had hidden it—one floor above, in the basement.

Salvatore drove his machine home, turned it into a corn popper, and sold it to an ice cream parlor.

Solution to "The Case of Bugs Meany, Thinker"

Bugs didn't want to return the cut-glass lamp. So he made up the story about the lamp being broken.

He said he was riding with it in the cargo space of his uncle's truck. Suddenly the truck stopped for a traffic light. That meant the truck was traveling forward.

But Bugs said the lamp "flew back over the tailgate."

When a truck (or any vehicle) comes to a sudden stop, objects inside it are pitched in the same direction in which the truck has been traveling.

So the lamp wouldn't have been thrown "back." It would have been thrown *forward!*

Tripped by his own words, Bugs returned the lamp to Winslow.

Solution to "The Case of the Grape Catcher"

According to Edsel, he'd been tied up in the garden hose for "hours and hours" instead of just a few minutes. He completely forgot that cold water had been passing through the hose and into the swimming pool before he was bound!

Had Edsel been telling the truth, the water standing in the hose would have been warm — having been under the hot sun for "hours and hours."

To prove Edsel lied, Encyclopedia turned on the hose for Officer Carlson. The water that came out had not yet had time to be heated by the sun. It was still cool.

Edsel's parents were informed. They squashed his grape catching for a year.

Solution to "The Case of the Left-Handers Club"

The guilty man was not really a lefty. He simply posed as a lefty in order to join the club and cause trouble.

However, he continued to use his right hand when he was alone—for example, when he *shaved.*

A left-handed man will almost always cut his left sideburn higher (shorter) than his right sideburn when he shaves. A right-handed man will cut his right sideburn higher.

Mike Dent's right sideburn was higher than his left!

The meaning did not escape Encyclopedia. He told the president of the Left-Handers Club. Mike Dent was secretly watched.

Three days later, the right-handed Mike was thrown out of the club.

Solution to "The Case of the Diving Partner"

Helga thought that if Otis, Encyclopedia, and Sally saw her getting out of the pond, they would be fooled. They would believe her lie that she had been in the water for "a solid hour."

However, she overlooked Encyclopedia's sharp eye for clues.

Remember that when she tapped her fingers together, Helga unmindfully called attention to her smooth skin? That was her downfall.

After an hour in the water, the skin would have been wrinkled!

Trapped by her own fingertips, Helga retired from the diving business.

She said the work was too hard.

Solution to "The Case of the Upside-Down Witness"

Elton said he had read two words on a sign in a store window while looking into a mirror and standing on his head. So the detectives looked for a sign with two words written upside down and backward.

They didn't find them.

That made Encyclopedia realize the truth. The two words could be read in the normal way—*and* upside down and backward!

The two words were on the fish store sign. They were CHOICE COD.

Encyclopedia told his father. The fish store was where the holdup was planned, and where the money was hidden. Within two days, the police had rounded up the gang.

Solution to "The Case of the Marvelous Egg"

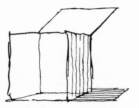

Wilford didn't have a square egg in the small box.

In fact, he didn't have anything. Every word was a lie. He made up the entire story about a square egg.

Still, he might have succeeded in fast-talking the children out of their money. However, he made one mistake. He said that Buddy Stilwell was "dressed and ready to jump."

The children were fooled, but not Encyclopedia. He saw that Buddy wore only one parachute.

A skydiver always jumps with *two* parachutes. The second is used in an emergency.

When Encyclopedia pointed out the mistake, the children left the dump without buying a single share.

Solution to "The Case of the Overfed Pigs"

The teen-ager was named Jim Hearn. He had been secretly fattening Lucy's pigs because he wanted his own pigs to star at Submarine World.

When Lucy's family returned from the movies, he was telephoning his friend to ask for a tow—his car had broken down. In his haste to escape from the house, he had dropped the slip of paper.

On the paper he had typed the telephone number of the place where his friend would be that night. Being careful, he had written the number in letters.

Pig iron on a telephone dial is the same as the number 744-4706, Encyclopedia realized.

The police traced the number. Jim and his friend were arrested.

Solution to "The Case of the Ball of String"

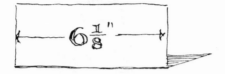

The thief rolled the ball of string out the back door, where he had a wheelbarrow waiting. He didn't want Cosimo to win the Collecting for Fun category.

First, however, he made sure that he could get the ball of string through the narrow door. He measured both the doorway and the ball.

The only measuring unit he had was a dollar. It is 6.14 inches long, but appears as 6 $\frac{1}{8}$ inches on a ruler. Because he didn't have a pencil, he scratched off the widths with a key.

The boy who "knew everything" about money certainly knew what spaces 6 $\frac{1}{8}$ inches apart were — the length of a dollar.

When he pretended not to know, Encyclopedia realized he — John Morgan — was the thief.

As a result, John was forced to withdraw his hobbies from the show. Cosimo's ball of string won the Collecting for Fun prize.

Solution to "The Case of the Thermos Bottle"

Bugs did not use the large thermos bottle. So why had he brought it to the carnival?

Encyclopedia got Miss Spottswood to examine the winning Ping-Pong ball. As he had suspected, the ball was cold.

Bugs had marked the ball at home and put it into the freezer for two hours. He brought it to the carnival in the thermos bottle to keep it cold.

Shortly before noon, he slipped the cold ball into the box with the other balls. Duke Kelly felt around till he found it.

Rick Larsen gave back the glove. Another drawing was held—without Bugs. Benny Breslin won.